One Cold Night

CLAIRE EWART

G. P. Putnam's Sons • New York

March 2001

For Ruth, My Warmest Wishes for your
own good words
and inspired photos.
love, Claire Ewart
Thanks!

For Tom, my love and my best friend

———————————————————

Copyright © 1992 by Claire Ewart. All rights reserved.
This book, or parts thereof, may not be reproduced in
any form without permission in writing from the publisher.
G. P. Putnam's Sons, a division of The Putnam & Grosset Group,
200 Madison Avenue, New York, NY 10016. Published simultaneously in Canada.
Printed in Hong Kong by South China Printing Co. (1988) Ltd.
Designed by Gunta Alexander.
Library of Congress Cataloging-in-Publication Data
Ewart, Claire.   One cold night/by Claire Ewart.   p.   cm.
Summary: Snow Woman tucks the animals in for the winter.
[1. Snow–Fiction. 2. Hibernation–Fiction. 3. Animals–Fiction.
4. Winter–Fiction.] I. Title.   PZ7.E9470n   1992   [E]–dc20   91-30879   CIP   AC
ISBN 0-399-22341-X
3   5   7   9   10   8   6   4   2

One cold night,

the cloud coyotes howled in the moonlight,

and Snow Woman came to tuck us in.

The birds huddled
as she brushed the last leaves from the trees,

the turtles burrowed as she stilled the stream,

the groundhogs hid as she frosted the fields.

But Black Bear didn't care.

So Snow Woman touched some moonbeams
and made the forest gleam.

She gathered frozen pinecones
and built a frozen fire.

She sent the fire northward and lit the sky ablaze.

Still Black Bear wouldn't leave.

So Snow Woman called the cloud coyotes,
and they scampered from the sky.

She sent them chasing Black Bear.

He scrambled for his den.

Then . . . Snow Woman tucked us in.